Taltal Levi was born in the Galilee, Israel. She graduated from Lucerne University of Arts and Design with a degree in illustration, and currently works and lives in Basel, Switzerland. From a young age she used drawing as a tool to liberate herself from reality's hardship and dullness. Taltal loves telling stories about characters who embrace their vulnerabilities and overcome obstacles. Her narratives incorporate fantasy elements and draw inspiration from nature, animals, and her own childhood memories.

To Jojo — T.L.

First published in the United States, Great Britain, Canada, Australia, and New Zealand in 2020 by NorthSouth Books Inc., an imprint of NordSüd Verlag AG, CH-8050 Zürich, Switzerland.

Distributed in the United States by NorthSouth Books Inc., New York 10016.

Library of Congress Cataloging-in-Publication Data is available.
Printed at Livonia Print, Riga, Latvia, 2020.
ISBN: 978-0-7358-4432-2
1 3 5 7 9 • 10 8 6 4 2

www.northsouth.com

MEET ME BY THE SEA

TALTAL LEVI

North South

Sometimes I feel invisible to the world,

so I go to my favorite place

where every tree and every bush is familiar,

and my feet get lighter with every step.

Things appear . . .

. . . and disappear.

Everything looks different in the dark,

and my feet get lighter with every step.

Things appear . . .

but I've come prepared.

Still, the night feels so vast and endless,

and I feel so small.

Others awaken,

while I drift off.

As morning breaks,

a surprise awaits.

Shy yet curious, just like me.

Perhaps I am not invisible after all?

A salty breeze washes our faces.

We are here!

I want to share something.

This is my favorite place, and these are my favorite people.

Just then . . .

Thank you for meeting me by the sea.